Disney's CHIP 'N DALE RESCUE RANGERS

The Rescue Rangers Save Little Red

By Betty Birney

Illustrated by Don Williams

A GOLDEN BOOK • NEW YORK

Western Publishing Company, Inc., Racine, Wisconsin 53404

Chip and Dale went to the circus.
They went to see Big Red.
Big Red was a clown.
They waited and waited.
The circus did not begin.
"There will be no show today,"
said the ringmaster.

"Little Red is missing,"
said a mouse.
Little Red was Big Red's dog.
Little Red did tricks.
"Big Red is very sad,"
said the mouse.

"We must find Little Red,"
said Chip.
"Then the circus can go on!"
cried Dale.

Big Red sat inside a tent.
He was crying.
"Where is Little Red?"
he said.

"I saw a cat,"
said the ringmaster.
"The cat was fat."
"Oh, no," said Chip and Dale.
"FAT CAT!"

The Rangers went to Fat Cat's place.
They listened outside the door.
"I sold Little Red to another circus,"
Fat Cat said.

He laughed.
"The circus is across the sea.
Little Red is at sea now,"
he said.
"He is on his way to the new circus."

"Fat Cat makes me mad!"
whispered Monterey Jack.
He pushed on the door.
The door opened.
Monterey Jack fell
into Fat Cat's room!

The rats put Monterey Jack in a cage.
"This little bird will not fly away,"
said Fat Cat.
Fat Cat laughed.

The Rangers went to the window.
"Oh, no!" said Gadget.
"We must save Monterey Jack,"
said Chip.

"I have an idea," said Gadget.
"I saw this trick in the circus."

Gadget opened the lock.
Monterey Jack was safe again.
"We must go to sea,"
said Chip.
"We must find Little Red,"
said Dale.

"We can try out my new boat,"
said Gadget.
"Is it safe?"
asked Dale.
"We will see,"
said Gadget.
The Rangers set sail.

The Rangers saw a balloon
in the sky.
It was big and red.
"There is Little Red,"
cried Chip.
"He is hanging from the balloon!"

"Little Red is so high up,"
said Dale.
"We can use our sail
for a kite!"
answered Gadget.

21

"Do not be afraid,"
Chip called to Little Red.
"We will save you,"
called Gadget.
Gadget handed Zipper a big pin.

"POP!" went the balloon.
Little Red fell
down, down, down.
Little Red was happy.
Fat Cat was not happy.

Fat Cat turned his boat
straight toward
the little boat.

26

CRASH! The big boat hit
the little boat.
"Help!" cried Monterey Jack.

"Hold on!" said Chip.
They floated
up, up, up on the kite.
Then they fell
down, down, down.
"Look!" said Chip.
"A ship!"

The ship saved them.
They sailed back to land.
"This is more fun
than the circus!"
said Little Red.

Big Red was happy
to see Little Red.
Now the circus could begin.
"More! More!"
the people shouted.
The Rangers were proud.

"That was a lot of work,"
said Chip.
"That was a lot of fun!"
said Dale.
Everyone cheered.